FRONT ROW SEAT

Published by Ladybird Books Ltd 2008
A Penguin Company.
Penguin Books, 80 Strand, London WC2R 0RL, UK

www.speedracerthemovie.com

ISBN 978-1-84646-957-2

10 9 8 7 6 5 4 3 2 1

Go, Speed Racer, Go!

Adapted by Sophia Kelly

Based upon the film *Speed Racer* written by The Wachowski Brothers.

PART I

CHAPTER ONE

Ten-year-old Speed Racer sat in his classroom taking a maths test. But his mind was elsewhere. All he could think about were race cars and the Thunderhead Raceway. His older brother, Rex Racer, was at the racetrack today. Speed wanted to be there watching his brother. But instead of having fun, Speed was stuck in school taking a multiple-choice test.

Speed looked at one of the questions: *Grace buys a bag of*

240 jelly beans. There are 35 yellow ones, 52 red ones, 63 green ones, 26 white ones, 41 blue ones and 40 black ones. If Grace wants to eat one of each while keeping her eyes closed, what is the minimum number she will have to eat? Speed looked up at the clock. He only had a minute left and didn't have a clue about how to work out the answer.

Then, all of a sudden, he had an idea. Speed quickly filled in all of the ovals with his sharp pencil just as the bell rang.

"All right, pencils down, bring your tests to the front," the teacher said.

Speed jumped up and slipped his test on her desk. He was halfway out the door before she even looked up.

"Speed Racer, slow down!" she called after him.

The next morning, the teacher sat down with Speed's mum for a meeting.

"Mrs. Racer," said the teacher. "Your son seems to be interested in only one thing. All he talks about is car racing."

"Well, you know," said Mom Racer. "His father designs racing cars."

"And where is your husband?" asked the teacher. She looked at the empty seat next to Mom Racer.

"He's . . . working," replied Mom Racer. "He couldn't make it."

The teacher asked, "Tell me, is your husband's name Rex?"

"No," said Mom Racer. "Rex is Speed's older brother. Why?"

Speed's teacher frowned. She held up Speed's test. Mom Racer looked at it and sighed. Speed had filled in the ovals so that they spelled out the phrase "Go, Rex, Go!"

CHAPTER TWO

The final school bell rang later that day. Speed raced out of class. He slid down the railing and burst through the front doors of the school. Rex was waiting for him in front of the school. Speed sprinted across the street. He jumped into the passenger seat of his brother's car and buckled himself in.

"I take it you're ready to go," said Rex. Speed nodded. Rex turned the key and revved the engine. The Racer brothers were off.

"So how was school?" Rex asked as they drove down the busy street.

"Fine," said Speed, but he had other things on his mind. "Are you going to the track? Mum said you were. You don't have to drop me off at home.

I could just go with you."

"No way," said Rex. "Pops would kill me."

"He doesn't have to know. I won't say anything. Come on, please, Rex. Pleeeease?" Speed begged.

"All right," Rex finally agreed. Then he steered the car towards the Thunderhead Raceway.

"Whoa!" shouted Speed as Rex's car zoomed down the racetrack. It felt like

he was on a roller coaster ride. But this time Speed wasn't in the passenger seat. He was sitting on his brother's lap, actually steering the race car around the track.

"Feel that shimmy?" Rex asked. "That's your hind legs trying to outrun your front."

"What do I do?" Speed asked.

"Stop steering and start driving," his brother answered. "A car isn't just a piece of metal. It's a living, breathing thing. She's alive. You can feel her

talking to you, telling you what to do. You just have to listen. Close your eyes and listen."

Speed closed his eyes and listened to Rex's voice.

"Ben Burns drove the last lap of the '68 Vanderbilt Cup with his eyes closed," continued Rex.

"No way!" Speed exclaimed.

"No? Well, maybe you can't hear what this car is telling you. Maybe you ought to be doing your homework instead..."

"No!" Speed interrupted. "I hear it!"

"That so? OK, then. Tell me when to punch it for the jump."

Speed kept his eyes shut and tried to concentrate as hard as he could.

"Now?" Rex asked.

"Not yet," said Speed. He waited just a few more seconds. It was as if the car was leading him towards the jump. "Now!"

WHOOSH!

Rex slammed on the accelerator pedal. The car was airborne. It glided over the jump as the Racer brothers steered the car together.

The next time Speed went to the track, he was there to watch Rex compete in the Thunderhead Race. Speed smiled. His brother was pulling into the lead.

Next to Speed, Pops Racer checked

his stopwatch.

"He's gonna win it," Speed said confidently. "He's gonna set the course record. Nobody's gonna catch him."

"Quiet, Speed," said Pops. "There's still a lot of race to run."

But that didn't stop Speed from saying aloud what he already knew. "It's over. My brother's the best racer in the world. Everybody else is running for second."

And sure enough, Speed was right. That night Rex won the race *and* set a new record for the course.

CHAPTER THREE

Watching his brother win at the Thunderhead Raceway was the best night of Speed Racer's life. But things didn't stay perfect for very long. A few days later, Speed sat on Rex's bed. He watched as his older brother packed a suitcase.

"Can I come, too?" asked Speed.

"Not this time, Speedy," Rex said.

"When are you coming back?" Speed asked.

"I don't know," answered Rex. "But there's something I want you to have."

Rex pulled out his keyring. He handed his car keys to Speed.

"But the Mach 5's your car!" said Speed.

"Not anymore," said Rex. He scooped up his younger brother in a big hug.

Rex let go of Speed and walked to the door. Pops was there waiting.

"So you really are quitting our team?" he asked angrily.

"I have to," replied Rex, calmly.

"No, you don't," Pops said. "This is a choice. You're selling out. You're

 walking away from everything our family has

built."

Rex sighed and walked towards the door. "I'm done fighting with you, Pops."

"Don't you walk away from me!" Pops yelled.

"You can't tell me what to do. It's my life to live," said Rex. He opened the door.

"If you walk out that door, you better not ever come back," cried Pops. But the only answer Pops got was the slam of the door.

It was the last time any of the Racers saw Rex.

PART II
Eight Years Later . . .

CHAPTER FOUR

VROOM!

The race cars roared down the track and the stands were full of race fans. People from all over the world were watching from home on television. They all wanted to know which driver would come in first in the Thunderhead Race.

The race cars weaved in and out of the pack. Each driver was trying to take the lead. Some of the cars even soared through the air around the tight curves. But no matter how many tricks the drivers pulled, no one could catch the Mach 6 and its driver – Speed Racer. Eight years had gone by since Rex had won this same race. Now it was Speed's chance to prove himself behind the wheel.

Way up above the track, the

announcers gave the play by play.

"Speed Racer, a local fan favourite, is gobbling up this track," the local announcer said into his microphone.

"No one seems able to lay a glove on this kid!" shouted the Australian announcer.

The Japanese announcer continued. "A win tonight could put him within range of qualifying for the Grand Prix!"

The crowd was going wild out in the stands. But Speed felt calm and confident as he sat inside the Mach 6. Racing was in his blood. And that's why he didn't lose his cool when Sparky, the Mach 6's mechanic, yelled into Speed's headset.

"Heads-up, Speed!" Sparky

exclaimed. "Snake's coming up from behind."

Speed glanced in his rearview mirror. Snake Oiler's orange and black car was bumper to bumper with the car directly behind the Mach 6. "Don't worry, Sparky," Speed said. "I got him."

As the race cars rounded the next turn, Snake Oiler slingshot his car in the direction of the Mach 6. Speed pressed a button on his steering wheel. The Mach 6 shot up high above the track on a set of jacks.

Snake's car slid underneath the Mach 6 and bounced

SMASH!

BOOM!

against

the guardrail. As it

skidded back towards Speed's car,

Speed steered the Mach 6 right into

Snake's car. Speed sent Snake's car

spinning and then took his chance to

pull even further forwards. The crowd

erupted in cheers and applause.

"Great move!" Sparky yelled into

the headset. "Holy cannoli, Speed.

You know whose record you

might beat?"

"Yeah . . ." said Speed, gazing out

the front window. Rex Racer had set

the record for this race eight

years ago.

"It's unbelievable, folks!" exclaimed the local announcer, jumping out of his seat. "No one's seen moves like this since that remarkable night eight years ago."

"There's no doubt about it in my mind," hollered another announcer. "Speed Racer is gunning for the record."

CHAPTER FIVE

Everyone in the stands watched with amazement as Speed Racer flew around each turn. He barely even stepped on the brakes. But there was one group of fans who had a personal interest in Speed's driving – the Racer family.

Pops lowered his binoculars and checked his stopwatch.

"Jeepers, he could do it, Pops," said Speed's younger brother, Spritle. "He could really do it, couldn't he?"

But Pops simply put the binoculars back up to his eyes.

"What if he does?" Spritle continued. "What if he does it, Pops?"

"SHH!" Pops warned. This race was too important to be spent chatting.

"I don't know if I can watch this . . ." said Spritle. He was more nervous than he'd ever been. He couldn't wait for the whole world to know what he knew – that Speed

Racer was going to set the new record at the Thunderhead Raceway! As Spritle put down his binoculars, a large hairy paw grabbed them from him.

"Chim-Chim!" Spritle cried, turning towards the Racer family's pet chimpanzee. "Those are *my* binoculars."

CHAPTER SIX

The race cars gunned their engines for the final lap, but there was no hope. Speed was too far in the **ROAR!** lead. There was no doubt that Speed would win this race. The only question now was whether he would beat his brother's record.

"He's coming hard," the local announcer cried. Speed was almost at the finish line. "It's gonna be close."

"This is gonna be *his* night," said another announcer.

"He's set to erase the record held by his brother," said the Australian announcer.

When the Mach 6 was only a few metres from the finishing line, Speed took his foot off the accelerator. That slowed him down a fraction of a second. The checkered flag went down. Speed had won the race!

But he hadn't beaten his

brother's record.

The crowd sighed. Everyone was disappointed that they hadn't seen Speed break the record. Everyone, that is, except for Speed's family. Their son was still the winner!

"Come on, let's go!" cried Spritle. "Victory lane."

Speed's family tore through the crowd to congratulate him.

"What a race!" said the French announcer.

"Incredible finish," the Japanese announcer agreed.

"Unbelievable," the German announcer chimed in. "Split-second late."

"And the record still stands," said the Australian announcer.

Finally, the local announcer spoke. "Folks, I knew Rex Racer and if he's somewhere watching this race, you can bet he's very proud of his little brother."

At the victory lane, cheering fans surrounded the Mach 6. Speed beamed. He had won the race *and* his big brother still had the record.

Everyone watching could tell that Speed was destined to be a great race car driver. Perhaps one day he would even compete in the world's most famous race – the Grand Prix! He may not have set a new record that night, but one thing was clear it was Speed Racer's time to shine!